To my pups, Milkshake and my late Wilfredo,
thank you for being my beloved muses
—L. C.

BEACH LANE BOOKS
An imprint of Simon & Schuster Children's Publishing Division
1230 Avenue of the Americas, New York, New York 10020
Text © 2023 by Cynthia Rylant
Illustration © 2023 by Lisa Congdon
Book design by Sonia Chaghatzbanian © 2023 by Simon & Schuster, Inc.
All rights reserved, including the right of reproduction in whole or in part in any form.
BEACH LANE BOOKS and colophon are trademarks of Simon & Schuster, Inc.
For information about special discounts for bulk purchases, please contact Simon & Schuster Special Sales at 1-866-506-1949 or business@simonandschuster.com.
The Simon & Schuster Speakers Bureau can bring authors to your live event. For more information or to book an event, contact the Simon & Schuster Speakers Bureau at 1-866-248-3049 or visit our website at www.simonspeakers.com.
The text for this book was set in Museo 500.
The illustrations for this book were rendered digitally.
Manufactured in China
1222 SCP
First Edition
10 9 8 7 6 5 4 3 2 1
Library of Congress Cataloging-in-Publication Data
Names: Rylant, Cynthia, author. | Congdon, Lisa, illustrator.
Title: Rain / Cynthia Rylant ; illustrated by Lisa Congdon.
Description: First edition. | New York : Beach Lane Books, [2023] | Audience: Ages 0-8. | Audience: Grades 2-3. |
Summary: "Children, animals, and natural life react to a coming rainstorm that will nourish them all"— Provided by publisher.
Identifiers: LCCN 2021059084 (print) | LCCN 2021059085 (ebook) | ISBN 9781442465091 (hardcover) | ISBN 9781442465107 (ebook)
Subjects: CYAC: Rain and rainfall—Fiction. | LCGFT: Picture books.
Classification: LCC PZ7.R982 Rai 2023 (print) | LCC PZ7.R982 (ebook) | DDC [E]—dc23
LC record available at https://lccn.loc.gov/2021059084
LC ebook record available at https://lccn.loc.gov/2021059085

written by Cynthia Rylant   illustrated by Lisa Congdon

Rain

Beach Lane Books • New York London Toronto Sydney New Delhi

There is a softness
and a quiet
before the rain comes.

The birds fly in with weather reports,
and the trees whisper with their leaves
to the squirrels:

Hurry home, friends.

Hurry home.

The squirrels come home.

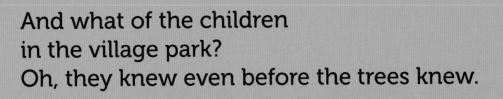

And what of the children
in the village park?
Oh, they knew even before the trees knew.

They watched as the sky changed
and the sun folded itself
into a cloud bed
while everything went gray.

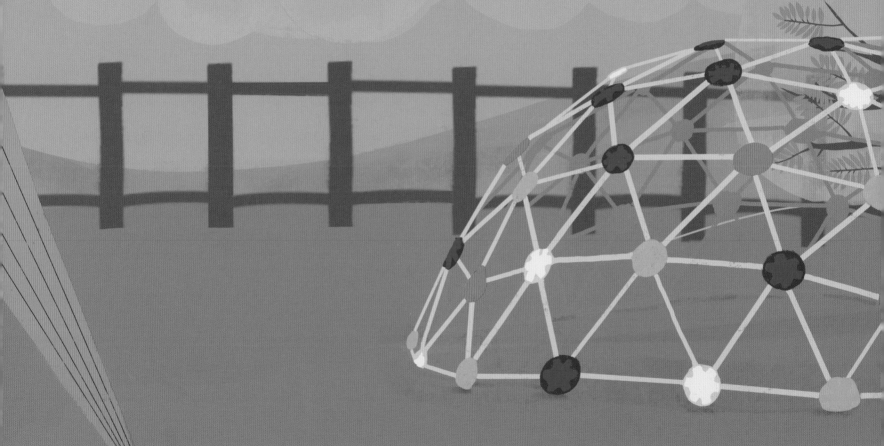

Time to hurry home, children.

Hurry home.

The children come home.

And the cats under rosebushes,
the cats on fences:
Do they know?

Oh, yes.
Their whiskers tell them so.

Cats love the rain,
but only from a windowsill
inside a safe, warm house.

So the cats lift their pretty tails
and hurry home.

And the dogs who have been
busy chewing bones
in friendly backyards:
Do they know about the rain?

The dogs knew even before the cats knew,
for the dogs' noses knew *yesterday*,
and the dogs have been waiting for the rain
all day long.

And will the dogs hurry anywhere?

Well, some fluffy ones might
squeeze under the porch.

And some long ones might
squeeze into the shed.

But most dogs will stay
right there in the yard
and wait for the first wet drops
on their noses.
Just for fun!

Then they will scratch at the kitchen door and find their friends.

And who is most happy about the rain?

Oh, the ducks of course.
They can't wait.
They paddle and paddle
and spread the word.

Mama ducks gather up the babies
and promise them
a *glorious* day!

And it is!
A glorious day.

The first wet drops
fall and bounce
on leaves,
on roofs,
on little birdhouses
with someone inside.

More rain,
heavier rain,
louder rain falls.

And it **is** glorious!

The birdbaths fill up.

The creeks fill up.

The dogs' best
water bowls fill up.

Wonderful,

free rain.

The trees enjoy their shower.

The cats have a show.

The dogs get cuddled.

And birds catch up on the news.

Rain is good for everybody!

And after it stops falling
and the sun starts to shine,
flowers will grow even taller,
gardens will grow more beans,
and every living thing
will be better.

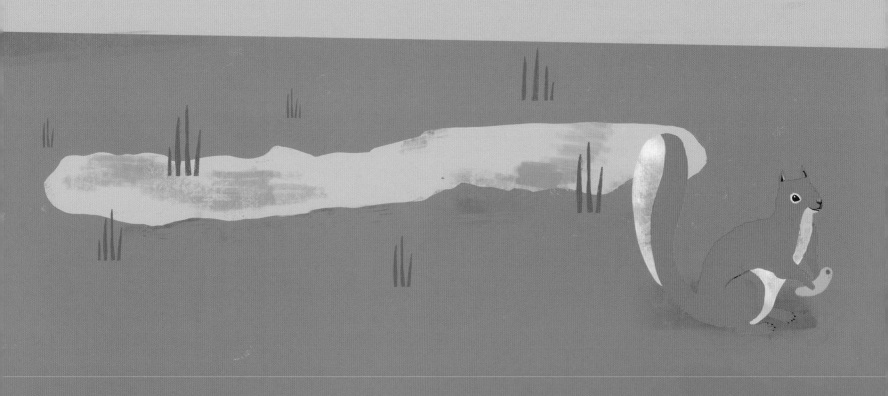

All because
of rain.